BENNY
Makes A Call

by Annette Nardone

*This book is dedicated to my four favorite people,
Dick, Sammy, Nikki & Kristy.*

Illustrated by Don Berry

Join Benny on one of his many historical adventures!

Look for these symbols throughout the story to learn important actual facts surrounding the events leading up to one of the greatest days in our history.

On August 10, 1876 Alexander Graham Bell made the first official long distance call from Brantford, Ontario Canada to Paris, Ontario Canada.

"Maaabel!" shouted Benny into the can. "Can you feel it?"

Mabel felt the can tremble next to her ear.

She couldn't answer him because she couldn't hear him. She was deaf.

"Maaabel!" yelled Benny again.

Just as Mabel tugged, a man came
out of nowhere and walked right
into the string.

"Aaaahh!" he yelled. "What's this?"

He sat on the ground looking at
the mess of string and cans tangled
around his legs. He began to laugh.
He loosened the strings and walked
away, still chuckling.

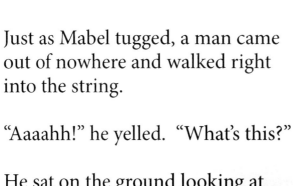

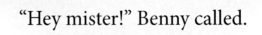

"Hey mister!" Benny called.

The man didn't hear Benny and kept
walking away …with their string and cans.

"Maaabel! Follow that guy!" shouted
Benny, pointing at
the stranger.

Like two detectives, Benny and Mabel slowly crawled up to a window. They climbed a huge tree to see inside. They could see perfectly when they hung by their legs from the branches. The table was covered with weird gadgets and gizmos.

"Wow Mabel, look at all that stuff. We'll never find our cans in all that mess."

Suddenly Mabel waved her arms and pointed to something on the end of the workbench. Their string can toy!

"Maybe there's a way to sneak in and get our toy back," said Benny. "If I swing I might be able to see better."

Benny swung his body back and forth, back and forth, back and forth. His long ears flapped in the breeze. "Just a little bit….. Aaaaaaaah! he shouted. Benny swung right off the branch and sailed through the window.

CRASH!! SMASH!! BANG!!

When Benny opened his eyes, he was staring at a pair of really big feet. He looked up.

"Well, hello there! Thanks for dropping in," said the man who had taken their toy.

Suddenly there was a scream from outside. Mabel was still hanging in the tree. Her skirts had fallen over her head!

"It seems that your friend has a little problem," said the man laughing.

Together they got a chair and rescued Mabel from her petticoat prison.

"By the way, I'm Alexander Bell, Aleck for short. What are your names?"

"I'm Benny and this is Mabel."

"Hello Benny," said Aleck. "Hello Mabel."

Mabel was shy. She was busy checking the dirt on her boots. She didn't see that Aleck was talking.

"She can't hear you," explained Benny. " She can understand most of what we say by watching us talk."

Aleck touched Mabel's hand and Mabel looked up.

"Hello Mabel. I'm Aleck," he said smiling.

She smiled back. "Thank you Aleck for helping me get down," Mabel said slowly.

"You are very welcome," Aleck said in a clear voice. "Mabel, you are very clever to be able to speak without hearing. I am a teacher in Boston and I help many deaf children learn to talk. How would you both like to come in? Only this time, let's use the door. I'd hate for you to hurt yourselves. Remember, curiosity killed the cat! Good thing you're a rabbit," he chuckled.

"Wow! Look at this place. Look at all the cool stuff," said Benny.

"These are my inventions," Aleck said.

"What do all these things do?" asked Benny.

"Right now I'm working on something very special. It's like a telegraph machine. The telegraph taps out sounds that spell words so that people can speak to each other from very far away," Aleck began.

"Can you talk to anyone, anywhere?" Benny asked excitedly. "Can you even talk to the Queen of England?"

Aleck held up his hands and laughed at Benny. "Slow down. Let me explain. A telegraph sends messages across wires using a code. If you don't know the code, it only sounds like a clicking noise. Telegraph operators are trained to listen to the code and translate the message. But what I am working on is even better. With my friend, Thomas Watson, I have figured out a way to send a human voice across the wires. It has never been done before. I call my invention – a telephone."

Benny scratched his head. "Hmmmmmm, seems like we invented something a lot like that telephone ourselves. Don't you agree Mabel? There it is too!" Benny exclaimed.

"Well, I'll be," laughed Aleck as he pulled down their cans and string and handed back their toy.

"So far, my invention is a lot like your toy. It has only worked from a short distance. I was just about to see if my telephone can send a voice message from one city to another?" Aleck asked.

"I'm sure it can!" said Benny.

"I'm sure, too!" said Mabel, slowly.

Aleck smiled. "Come on then. I'm going to need some help with this," Aleck said.
"My idea is to take the receiver to Paris!"

"But that's eight miles away!" cried Benny. "How can we get it there?"

"We can run the wires along the fences until we connect them to the telegraph line on the main road. They hook up to the telegraph office in Brantford, " explained Aleck.

Benny and Mabel nodded and followed him outside. They watched Aleck run the wires until he came to a dead end. There was no more fence.

"I'm going to have to take the wires through this tunnel," he said, bending down to peer into the badger-sized hole. "Looks pretty muddy in there."

Aleck started to crawl into the tunnel. First, he jiggled his arms. Then, he wriggled his shoulders. Suddenly, all movement stopped. His head was wedged inside, but his bum was sticking out.

"Uh, anything wrong Aleck?" asked Benny.

"You could say that," said Aleck.

Benny and Mabel tried hard not to laugh at their friend.
"You're stuck, aren't you?" giggled Benny.

"You could say that," said Aleck.

Benny and Mabel each grabbed a leg. They pulled and pulled.
With one final tug, Aleck popped out and all three landed on
their backs laughing!

"Oh no! What will I do now?" asked Aleck.

"Let me try it," shouted Benny jumping up and down. "I can do it. I'm small enough. Please let me help you!"

"Thanks!" said Aleck as he handed Benny the wires. "Mabel and I will be at the other end waiting to help you out."

Benny slipped into the small opening. Before he was all the way in, he jumped back out.

"Th..th..there's something creepy in there," he said shivering and dripping with mud. "Millions of eyes were staring right at me."

Mabel took a lantern she had brought and shined it inside. Up against the wall of the tunnel was a family of raccoons.

"Go on, Benny," she said. "Those raccoons won't hurt you."

Benny grabbed the wires and made his way into the hole once more. He decided not to stop to chat with the furry bunch and quickly raced right through. "Made it!" Benny shouted as he popped out of the other end.

Aleck and Mabel laughed at the mud-caked rabbit. As the grimy group trudged into Paris, everyone in town stared.

"Hi there everyone," said Benny. "You've just got to come and see what my friend has invented. It's the most amazing thing!"

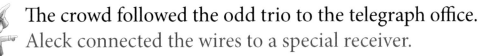 The crowd followed the odd trio to the telegraph office. Aleck connected the wires to a special receiver.

"Now off you go to Brantford. Go to the telegraph office there and send me the best message you can think of," Aleck said as he waved goodbye.

Benny and Mabel hitched a ride in a horse-drawn cart. A crowd of people followed close behind. Everyone wanted to know what was going on. They headed back to the telegraph office in Brantford. As they walked, the people asked Benny and Mabel hundreds of questions.

"Just wait and see, you'll be amazed!" Benny said.

At 8p.m. sharp, the crowd in the telegraph office went silent. **Benny leaned forward and spoke into the transmitter.**

"Aleck, can you hear me?" he asked.

"Hoy! Hoy!" shouted the crowd.

They had no way of knowing if Aleck could hear him. This telephone worked one way. "Hey, everybody! Let's try singing," Benny yelled.

They all sang.

"***Louder!***" shouted Benny. They crowd sang so loud that the office began to shake. Mabel could feel the vibrations through her feet. She began to dance. "***Louder!***" shouted Benny once more. They sang and sang until one by one they couldn't sing any more.

Mabel looked around at the silent faces. She stopped dancing and started to cry. "He can't hear us!" she wailed.

"Don't cry Mabel," said Benny. "Just wait and see."

Suddenly the telegraph machine started tapping. The operator quickly ran back to his seat and wrote down the message.

"Don't stop...It's the most beautiful music... Aleck..."

Everyone cheered and danced. ***"Hurray! It works!"***

A huge smile spread over Alexander Graham Bell's face as he listened into his receiver.

"Singing! They're all singing!" he said to himself. "The first long distance telephone call and they are all singing!"

ALEXANDER GRAHAM BELL

1847 Alexander Bell is born in Edinburgh, Scotland

1860 Bell moves to London, England to live with his grandfather

1861 Bell begins teaching in Elgin, Scotland

1864 Bell helps father demonstrate his Visible Speech system

1869 Bell starts teaching the deaf in London, England

1870 The Bell family emigrate to Canada

1871 Bell moves to Boston, Mass. to teach at the School for the Deaf Mutes

1872 Bell opens his own school for the deaf in Boston, Mass.

1873 Bell starts experimenting on the multiple telegraph

1874 Bell becomes Professor of Vocal Physiology at the Boston University

1875 Thomas Watson becomes Bell's assistant

1875 Watson and Bell manage to transmit the sound of a plucked reed

1876 On March 7, a patent for the telephone is issued to Bell
     On March 10, the first telephone message "Mr. Watson-come here-I want to see you" is heard in Boston, Mass., marking the
              "INVENTION OF THE TELEPHONE"
     On June 25, Bell demonstrates his telephone at the Centenary Exhibition in Philadelphia
     On August 10, the first long distance telephone call is made from Brantford, Ontario to Paris, Ontario-approximately 13 km
     On October 6, the first two-way conversation took place between Bell and Watson

1877 Bell marries Mabel Hubbard on July 11

1877 Bell Telephone Company is formed in the U.S.

1880 Bell invents Photophone. This uses light waves to send sound

1881 Bell invents a metal detector and a respirator

1888 Bell founds the National Geographic Society with his father Alexander Melville Bell.

1892 Bell makes his first long distance call in the U.S. from New York to Chicago

1893 Bell sets up the Association for the Promotion of Teaching Speech to the Dea

1908 Bell wins a prize for the first manned flight longer than 5/8 mile.
     The plane is called the June Bug

1915 Bell opens the first transcontinental telephone line from New York to San Francisco

1922 On August 2, Alexander Graham Bell dies. He is buried at Beinn Bhreagh, Nova Scotia in Canada. Every telephone falls silent for one minute in memoriam

1923 On January 3, Mabel dies and is buried next to Alexander.
     Mabel and Alexander had two daughters, Elsie May and Marian (Daisy). The also had two sons Edward and Robert but both died shortly after birth.